John
and
Tom

For information about permission to reproduce
selections from this book, write to

PERMISSIONS
THE VERMONT FOLKLIFE CENTER
MASONIC HALL
3 COURT STREET, BOX 442
MIDDLEBURY, VERMONT 05753

LIBRARY OF CONGRESS | CATALOGING-IN-PUBLICATION DATA
Lange, Willem, 1935-
    John and Tom / Willem Lange; illustrated by Bert Dodson.—1st ed.
        p. cm. — (The family heritage series)
    Summary: When John has an accident while cutting logs in the
Vermont woods, Tom, the Morgan horse who is his work partner and
friend, uses intelligence and strength to rescue him.
    ISBN 0-916718-17-4
    1. Morgan horse—Juvenile fiction. [1. Morgan horse—Fiction.
2. Horses—Fiction. 3. Lumbermen—Fiction. 4. Accidents—Fiction.
5. Logging—Fiction. 6. Vermont—Fiction.] I. Dodson, Bert, ill. II.
Title. III. Series.

PZ10.3.L344 Jo 2001
[Fic]—dc21   2001026032

ISBN 0-916718-17-4
Printed in Hong Kong, China
Distributed by Independent Publishers Group (IPG)
814 North Franklin Street, Chicago, IL 60610

FIRST EDITION

Book design: Sarah Kilkelly, Joseph Lee, Black Fish Design
Series Editor: William Jaspersohn

10 9 8 7 6 5 4 3 2 1

Publication of this book was made possible by a grant from the
Christian A. Johnson Endeavor Foundation.

Then there's the one about John and Tom.

John was a young logger who lived on a farm in
the hills with his mother and father. Tom was a
big, husky Morgan horse who helped John haul
logs from the woods. John often said that Tom
was the smartest horse in the world.

One cold morning in November, John packed
his lunch in his old lunch box. Then he put on
his rubber shoepacs, his mackinaw and his wool
hat, told his parents he'd be back before dark,
and went out to harness Tom.

Tom and John spoke to each other in their
own language when they were working. To some
people, the words all sounded strange. But to
John and Tom, each word meant something.
When John walked into the stable, Tom raised
his head and snorted, with a sound like a motor
running. That meant, "Good morning."

When Tom snorted, John said, "Hoy!" That meant, "Good morning." When John wanted Tom to go ahead, he said, "Hyup!" When he wanted the horse to stop, he said, "Ho!" To go to the left, he said, "Haw!" To go to the right, he said, "Gee!" Back up was "Heeyah!"

And if John wanted Tom to pull hard, he cried, "Hyah!" He never used reins to tell Tom what to do.

But every morning Tom played a little game. After John put on Tom's harness, the horse wouldn't move. He just stood there. John always said, "What's the matter, boy?" Tom blew his breath out and sniffed around John's pockets until he smelled what he was looking for: an apple. "Oh, so that's it!" John would say, pulling the apple out of his pocket.

Tom would crunch the apple in his teeth,
and off they would go to the woods, with the
long log chain dragging behind them.

That particular day, they worked all morning,
hauling logs out of the woods and into a pile.
At noontime they ate lunch. John put a feed bag
of grain over Tom's nose and sat down on a tree
stump to eat his sandwiches. Afterward, each
of them had an apple for dessert.

"Well, Tom," said John after lunch, "I'm going to tie you over there while I fell a few more."

John began to saw down more of the trees. As each one tumbled, he trimmed off its branches with his ax and sawed it into logs.

Then all at once something happened. One big white pine tree started to fall, then leaned against another tree. John had to get it down somehow. But a leaning tree is very dangerous; it can jump in any direction off its stump. John very carefully chopped at the cut between the trunk and the stump.

Suddenly, the big pine jumped sideways off its stump and drove down into the snow, pinning John's foot to the ground.

John knew his foot was hurt badly. He was sitting in the snow, but he couldn't move. What was he going to do? It was cold enough that he could freeze to death out there in the woods, and soon it would be dark, besides.

"Tom!" he called. "Come here, boy!" Tom tried to pull free. But his rope was tied too well, and he couldn't break it.

"Come on, boy!" said John again. Tom understood. He started to chew on the rope with his big teeth. In five minutes he was free. He shambled over, his chain dragging behind him.

"Ho," said John. Tom stopped. John tried to reach the chain. It was just out of reach.

"Heeyah!" he said. Tom backed up, and finally John could grab it. He wrapped the chain around the fallen tree. It was almost dark now and John was getting cold. "Tom," he said, "this tree is heavy, and I've got to get out of here. See if you can move it, boy. Hyup! Hyah!"

Tom pulled as hard as he could, moving from side to side, but the tree wouldn't budge. It was just too big for him. "Ho, boy," said Tom. "Heeyah! Let's try something else. Gee! Hyup!"

The horse seemed to know what he had to do. He turned his head and looked back at John. Then he dropped his belly to the ground and pulled as hard as he could, his great muscles bulging with the strain. His belly brushed the snow. He leaned. John could feel the tree stir just a tiny bit.

"Hyah!" he cried, and Tom gave one last tug. The tree moved again, and John yanked his foot out of the hole the tree had made in the snow.

"Ho!" called John. His foot throbbed. Tears filled his eyes, but they were not tears of pain.

"Good boy! Good boy, Tom. Heeyah! Let's get
that chain off you. I can't walk. I'm going to
have to ride out of here."

Tom stood still, looking back at John. John
grabbed hold of Tom's collar and pulled
himself up onto his back. "Hyup!" he said.
"Let's go home."

Back at the house, John's parents were worried. "He's never been this late before," fretted John's mother. "I just know something awful has happened. I should have told him not to go alone."

Tom's father was worried too. He put on his boots and coat, took a flashlight out of a drawer, went outside into the snow and started for the woods.

He'd gone only a little way before he heard
hooves softly clopping toward him in the
darkness. He shone the flashlight ahead of him,
and there was John and Tom, with John riding,
hanging on to Tom's collar with both hands.

"What happened to you, son?" asked John's father.

"A tree pinned me. I broke my foot. It really hurts. But Tom got me out all right."

"We knew you shouldn't go into the woods alone," John's father said. "From now on, you'll take a friend in case there's trouble."

"But Dad, I always take a friend. The best friend anybody could ever have!"

He patted Tom's big, thick neck and wiped away some snowflakes. Tom turned his head halfway around and snorted. He could tell he'd probably get an extra apple for dessert that night.

ANIMAL TALES

Family animals—dogs, cats, horses and others—often hold places of special importance in the families they live with. Some of these animals are pets, loved almost as family members. Others, like Tom in *John and Tom*, are work animals, valued for their intelligence, strength and reliability. Just like the humans in their lives, all of these animals can be the sources of wonderful stories—stories that can be told and passed on to younger generations.

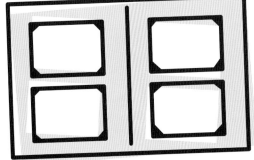

Make an animal scrapbook

How about you? Do you have stories about your pets, past and present? What about your parents, grandparents and other family members? Do they have animal stories?

Do this: Ask older friends or family members to tell you a tale about an animal from their past. To get the storytelling started, you might want to ask the person questions like these:

› Did your family have animals when you were a child? What did you have, and what were they like? What kinds of chores did you do for your animals?

› What were some of the most memorable things you and your pet did for fun?

› Did you ever have any adventures together?

› Did any of your animals ever do something amazing, heroic or funny?

› What about hunting and fishing stories? Or encounters with animals in the wild. Do you have any of those tales?

› Were there work animals or barn animals in your life when you were young? What did they do? How were they important to the families that had them?

Later you might want to start an animal scrapbook and write in it some of the animal stories you've heard. Paint or draw pictures to go with the stories. Add tales and pictures of your favorite pet or animal.

Give it a try. Become a collector, or archivist, of your family's animal tales!